For Mikayla, Jackson, Alice and Charlie, who love to read.

To my mother, Harriet Sherman, my greatest supporter,
who taught me to follow my dreams. –Joseph

Acknowledgements

For their keen reading and invaluable contributions, bear-sized thanks to Naomi Le Guédard, Anne Paradis, Emily Katz, Alice and Charlie Juenke, Mikayla and Jackson Conners, Stephanie Bolster, Madeleine and Éloïse Leroux, Kate Hall, Luka and Étienne Da Costa-Hall, Ann Lambert, Alyda Faber, Robin Budd and Anita Anand. Julia is lucky to have you as her friends, and so are we.

About the authors

Andrew has been writing, storytelling and teaching in Montreal for more than fifteen years. **Juliana's** first novel, *Nirliit*, was published in French in 2015. It was translated into English by Véhicule Press in 2018 and will be adapted for the screen. This is their first children's book.

About the illustrator

Joseph Sherman is a Gemini award-winning children's animation series director, with 30 years of experience in the design and production of animated series, motion graphics and print illustrations. This is his first picture book.

How To Catch A Bear Who Loves To Read is inspired by a real-life friendship between the two authors. It all started when Juliana joked that the best way to catch Andrew would be with books and cookies.

For the whole story, visit **crackboombooks.com**.

HOW TO CATCH A BEAR

who LOVES to READ

by Andrew Katz and Juliana Léveillé-Trudel
illustrated by Joseph Sherman

CRACKBOOM!

Julia had many friends in the forest by her house. She climbed trees with Scotty, played hide-and-seek with Abigail and had farting contests with Frieda.

Julia dreamed of meeting a bear. She wanted to raft
along the river on its belly and have a bearnormous
picnic together in the clearing.
And, of course, she wanted to give it a hug.
A bear hug!
But no bear ever showed its snout.

One morning, Julia was absorbed in a book. It was about a bear who set off on a long journey to visit a very dear friend.
Along the way, this bear felt his stomach rumble. He stopped to sniff through some bushes for a snack.
Julia looked up from her book, her eyes shining.
She had an idea.

She brought honey—which is a bear's favorite snack—
and waited for the sweet smell to blow through the trees.
Suddenly, there was a loud rustling in the bushes.
"YUMMMMM!" said a voice.
Julia spun around, her heart full of hope.

But it was only Scotty.
"That looks delicious!" he said.
"May I try some?"
Julia gave a little sigh and nodded.
And still, no bear.

The next morning, Julia carried another bear snack into the forest.
And because bears could play hard to get, she also brought her book.
She plunged back into the story: the bear was lending a helping paw
to an old turtle who was crossing the river.
As Julia turned the page, the trees shished.
SPLACK!
Julia jumped.

Next to the overturned basket stood Abigail.
"Sorry, Julia! I wasn't looking where I was going.
I'm playing hide-and-seek with Scotty and Frieda!"
Abigail helped Julia pick up some of the blueberries.
But still, no bear.

A familiar voice rang faintly through the forest.
Julia's mom was calling her for lunch.
"See you soon, Abigail!" said Julia to her friend.

A little later, Julia ran back to the forest to get her book.
But her book was gone.
Instead, on the ground, there was a funny looking paw print.
It was blueberry colored, and much bigger than any print
she'd ever seen.
Her heart did a somersault. Who'd made this?

She glanced in every direction.
Nobody.
But just ahead, another print,
blue like the first one.
And another. And another.
FFFBLRRRRRRRRRT!

"Hi, Julia!" said Frieda. "Ready for a farting contest?"
"Sorry, Frieda, I can't fart right now. I'm looking for someone!"
"Who?"
"That's what I have to find out!"

"Hey! Where are you two going?" said Abigail, scampering over with Scotty.

Frieda whispered, "Julia's on someone's trail, but she doesn't know whose."

The paw prints meandered down a gulley, up a hill, around a boulder and down again to the edge of a stream, where they disappeared.
"The water must have washed all the blueberry away," said Scotty.
"Now what do we do?" Julia said.
"Don't worry," said Abigail. "We're hide-and-seek champions!"

Frieda sniffed the air. "This way!"

Abigail pointed to a gap in some bushes. "Through here!"

Julia crept through the bushes and emerged near the foot of a very old tree.
"Look!" said Scotty.
Gigantic claw prints marked a path up the trunk.

Julia took a deep breath and grabbed the first branch.
"Are you sure you want to go up there?" Frieda said.
"I'll be careful," said Julia.
"I'll go with you," said Scotty. "Just in case."

Julia pulled herself up with a bear-like grunt.
One branch at a time, she clung and clambered
her way higher and higher.
"You climb as well as a squirrel!" said Scotty.

Julia ran into a big troublesome knot. She tried to scrape
and scramble her way around it. But she had no luck.
Even Scotty didn't know how to help her.
With a huff and a puff, she gathered all her strength for one
last try, and this time …
She made it.

At the top of the tree, she collapsed, out of breath.
"Julia, look!" said Scotty.
A house.
Nestled among the leaves was a house, its front door slightly ajar.
Julia's heart went BA-BOOM as she took a step forward.

"I'll wait for you here," Scotty squeaked. "If you need me, I'll be there in a jiffy."
Julia knocked softly. No answer.
She knocked loudly. Still no answer.
She peeked inside …

A bear.

On the floor, snoring peacefully, was a bear.

And books!

From the floor to the ceiling, shelves upon shelves
upon shelves of books.

And there, spread open on the chest of the bear: *her* book.

Julia's heart soared, and fluttered with just a little fear. She was standing in a bear's house, and she hadn't been invited in. But she couldn't leave without her book.

She tiptoed towards the bear and delicately lifted her book off his chest.
I'll come back later to introduce myself, she thought.
"Wait!" said a deep growly voice.
Julia froze.

"Please, wait! You are most welcome to that book. But first, may I please read the ending? I closed my eyes just before the bear reached his friend!"

Julia turned around and stared, amazed.

"That's … that's exactly the part I was reading!" she said. "But I didn't know bears liked to read."

"I love to read!" said the bear. "I'm always on the lookout for a good book."

"Of course, I only venture into the village when all the people are asleep. The best spot for book scavenging is by the back door of the library. The librarians there are kind enough to leave boxes of old books outside. Oh, the treasures I find as I rummage through them! But today, I found that book right here in the forest! A scent of blueberries tickled my nose and led me straight to it."

"It was me who brought those blueberries," said Julia. "And I left this book there, by accident."
She thought for a moment.
"Maybe we could finish reading it together?" she said.

"Splendid idea!" said the bear. "But where are my manners?
My name is Bertrand."
He held out his paw.
"And my name is Julia," said Julia, giving Bertrand's paw
a vigorous shake.
"There's a lovely reading spot out on the porch," said Bertrand.
"Make yourself at home and I'll join you in a twinkling."

Bertrand carried out two bowls of blueberries drizzled with honey.
"What an intriguing story," Bertrand said. "The bear journeys such
a long way to visit his friend."
"Because they're very dear friends," said Julia.

Julia and Bertrand savored the end of the book.
The trees whooshed gently. The dappled light, sweeping around
in the leaves, began to dim.
They read the last page.
A moment later, Julia's mom's voice echoed through the forest.
It was time to go home.

Bertrand showed Julia the best route to climb back down.
"What a fortunate acquaintance this has been!" he said.
"How about I bring a new book next time?" said Julia. "And afterwards, could we raft along the river? And go on a picnic?"
"Certainly!" said Bertrand.
"I just have one more question," Julia said.

"Can I give you a hug?"

The End

©2018 CHOUETTE PUBLISHING (1987) INC.

CrackBoom! Books is an imprint of Chouette Publishing (1987) Inc.

Text: Andrew Katz and Juliana Léveillé-Trudel
All rights reserved.
Illustrations: Joseph Sherman

Chouette Publishing would like to thank the Government of Canada and SODEC
for their financial support.

Canadä

Québec
Books
Tax Credit
Gestion
SODEC

Bibliothèque et Archives nationales du Québec and Library and Archives Canada
cataloguing in publication

Léveillé-Trudel, Juliana, 1985-, author

How to catch a bear who loves to read/text, Juliana Léveillé-Trudel and Andrew
Katz; illustrated by Joseph Sherman.

(CrackBoom! Books)
Issued also in French under title: Comment attraper un ours qui aime lire.
Target audience: For children aged 3 and up.

ISBN 978-2-924786-47-5 (hardcover)

I. Katz, Andrew, 1975-, author. II. Sherman, Joseph (Illustrator), illustrator.
III. Title.

PS8623.E944H6913 2018   jC813'.6   C2018-940667-4
PS9623.E944H6913 2018

CRACKBOOM! BOOKS

©2018 Chouette Publishing (1987) Inc.
1001 Lenoir St., Suite B-238
Montreal, Quebec H4C 2Z6 Canada
crackboombooks.com

Printed in China
10 9 8 7 6 5 4 3 2 1 CHO2042 JUL2018